PERFECTLY Fine

LJ EVANS

This book is a work of fiction. While reference might be made to actual historical events or existing people and locations, the events, names, characters, places, and incidents are either the product of the author's imagination or are used fictitiously, and any resemblance to actual persons, living or dead, business establishments, events, or locales is entirely coincidental.

PERFECTLY FINE © 2022 by LJ Evans

LJ EVANS BOOKS

www.ljevansbooks.com

Cover Design: © River Briar Designs
Cover Images: © iStock / hugolacasse / Andrii Vinnikov / Greens87 / Christos Georghiou
Copy Editor: Jenn Lockwood Editing Services

Printed in the United States

Playlist

https://spoti.fi/3jITlcJ

"Superstar" by Taylor Swift
"Nervous" by Maren Morris
"Message in a Bottle" by Taylor Swift
"Great Ones" by Maren Morris
"Space" by Maren Morris
"Back to December" by Taylor Swift
"Mr. Perfectly Fine" by Taylor Swift
"Bye Bye Bye" by Taylor Swift
"How You Get the Girl" by Taylor Swift

Dedication

To everyone who looked at the stars and wished for them to be yours.

May you reach out and grab one.

Chapter One
Gemma

SUPERSTAR
Performed by Taylor Swift

The red carpet was bare as Etta and I left the theater, but I was still giddy from the dream-like experience of attending my very first movie premiere—a movie I'd had a teeny-tiny hand in making. I made Etta stop in front of the poster to take a picture. We hadn't dared do it earlier when the place had been teeming with the press, fans, and celebrities.

I stared at the selfie for a minute, overcome with strong emotions. It was almost impossible to believe that the woman with her blonde hair piled on top of her head, hazel eyes gracefully layered in makeup, and slim body clad in a black satin slip-dress was actually me. The dress, with its hemline ending barely below my butt cheeks, wasn't one I would have ever bought, but I was grateful to Etta for loaning it to me.

"I can't believe this is me," I said, looking at her with a cheesy grin before hugging her. "I never expected Wilson to invite me to the premiere. I'm just some low-life assistant, scuttling to get him coffee."

"An assistant who pulled a rabbit out of a hat with the yellow-stoned tiara you found in the middle of Nowhere, Tennessee!" she said as her tightly laced braids danced around her.

While I looked nothing like my normal self tonight, Etta was as gorgeous as always in purple satin that accentuated her deep-brown shoulders. She looked like a movie star, even if she had no desire to be one. Instead, her head was full of numbers and marketing schemes.

"The original tiara getting lost in transit was the best thing to ever happen to me," I said, gratitude filling my heart. "Look at me now! Living in Hollywood with you! Working at the studio with the Wilson Devney! I think Great-Granny Mc would have gotten a kick out of her hoarding ways bringing me a step closer to my dreams."

"You're talented, Gemma. Your screenplay is absolutely going to find a home soon," Etta said.

I held my breath for a moment, thinking of all the queries I'd sent out. Rejection after rejection. But it only took one, and I wouldn't give up. Not ever. So what if right now I was barely scraping by? So what if I was living on a pull-out couch in Ella's one-room apartment? I was in Los Angeles. I had a fabulous new friend and a job where I got to see movie magic happen every day.

As Etta and I reached the curb, a black limousine pulled over in front of us. The window rolled down to reveal Wilson. His dark eyes were concerned, heavy eyebrows scrunching together in an ageless brown face.

"Etta! Gemma! What are you doing standing on the curb like you're waiting for a john to pick you up?" he groused, his booming voice carrying down the street.

My face flushed bright red, but Etta laughed.

"We're just waiting for the car we ordered. Don't get your panties in a bunch." Etta smiled.

The limo door opened, and Wilson waved us in. "Cancel it. There's plenty of room with us. Get in!"

Etta and I exchanged a look before crawling over Wilson's long legs into the back. It wasn't until we were seated that I realized it wasn't just Wilson and his husband in the car. My heart skipped about twenty beats before restarting at a wild pace. I inhaled sharply as my eyes met vivid, blue ones.

Rex Carter, A-lister and lead actor in *Wild River*, was in the flipping limousine with us! He looked magnificent in a black tuxedo cut and carved to fit every single chiseled muscle. The buttons on his jacket were open to reveal a black vest lined with silver threads that matched his silk tie. The neutral palette blended in with his black hair and tan skin, making the royal blue of his eyes stand out even more.

I'd never understood the phrase "so handsome it hurt" until I'd come face to face with Rex in real life. But every time I was within a twenty-foot radius of the man, my chest exploded into a thousand pieces. It was ridiculous. The awareness tingling through my veins threatened to turn me into the drooling fan I'd promised myself I'd never be.

Rex's left eyebrow raised, the perfectly arched black curve going even higher as I continued to stare. He had indecently kissable lips that were quirked upward at the moment, smoothing out the tiny scar at the corner. His eyes strolled down from my face to my body clad in Etta's tiny dress before landing at the juncture between my legs and staying there for a beat. My face flared again as I realized that between climbing over Wilson and sliding down the seat to make room for Etta, the dress had scrunched even higher up my thighs. Rex Carter was probably getting a clear shot of my neon-pink underwear.

"So, what do you think, ladies?" Wilson asked. "Are we going to win an Oscar?"

Wilson rubbed his hands together in excitement. His blond-haired husband—also in a tux but looking nowhere near as devastating as the actor sitting next to him—put a large hand on Wilson's leg. "You know you are. Stop fishing for more compliments."

Wilson's laugh thundered through the car, and Rex's grin turned into a full smile that made my frozen heart squeeze tight.

"I'm not sure Gemma agrees," Rex teased, and I lost feeling in half my body not only because of the way he said my name, deep and guttural, but because he actually knew it. Sure, I'd worked on set for eight weeks while they'd been filming on location in my hometown, but we'd never had a single conversation.

Etta elbowed me, the sharp edge digging into my ribcage, and the pain finally broke my gaze from Rex's. When I turned to her, Etta was frowning.

"Gemma totally agrees. Don't you? Not only is Wilson going to win Best Director, but Rex is going to win Best Actor. There are no doubts. Believe me, I've nailed the winners with an eighty-percent success rate for five years," Etta said.

I cleared my throat, forcing my heart to beat again before finally speaking. My voice came out breathy and soft in a way that made me want to cringe. "Wilson has Best Director in the bag, but Rex has competition with Ben Winters."

Wilson chuckled, and Etta shot me a glare. I shrugged at her but refused to meet Rex's eyes as they bored into me. I wasn't going to lie just to stroke his ego. He didn't need it stroked…certainly not by me. Pink hit my cheeks again because stroking and Rex were definitely not words I should combine, even in my head.

"What?" I said, looking at Etta instead of the man making my pulse spike. "It's the truth. Ben's performance in *Deadly Escape* was riveting."

"Ouch," Rex said. The humor in that one word drew my gaze back to his face where his delectable lips quirked even more. I was saved from responding as the limousine came to a stop in front of Wilson's mansion in the Hollywood hills.

Wilson clambered out, reaching in to help Greg and then Etta out of the vehicle. Rex stepped out on the other side and put his hand back in the car to assist me. When I hesitated before accepting it, a rumbling chuckle broke from deep inside his chest that did all sorts of things to my core.

"I promise, holding my hand for two seconds isn't going to kill you," he teased.

I rolled my eyes. "You're ridiculous."

The moment my palm slid into his, shock waves rippled through me, zapping along my veins and making me falter. His other hand went to my waist to steady me, and the gentle touch lit me up like a roadside flare. I needed help. I needed to send an

S.O.S. and hope someone would save me before I made a fool out of myself.

When I looked up into his face, towering above me even in my four-inch heels, his sexy smile had disappeared, and his eyes had turned stormy. His dark pupils were dilated, pushing his blue irises into tiny slivers.

Nerves had me biting the corner of my lip, and his gaze tracked the movement. His fingers on my waist flexed ever so slightly, easily digging into my skin through the barely-there dress.

Rex Carter was very, very wrong.

His touch could easily destroy me.

Chapter Two
Rex

My hand and gaze were stuck on frozen on Gemma's soft skin. I caught a hint of pink tongue as she licked her lips before she sank her teeth into the bottom one. I had the overwhelming desire to pull both into my mouth. To devour them. To devour her. The severity of my reaction was a puzzle I hadn't figured out, even after eight weeks of filming with her on set in Tennessee. I'd had a hard time tearing my eyes from her when she'd been wearing jeans, T-shirts, and Keds, and now that she was in a tiny black dress barely covering anything, it was damn near impossible.

It took a wild amount of control to drag my hands from her, and I instantly longed to put them back, to bask in the warmth of our bodies joined. She shivered in the unusually cool November air, and I wished she was quivering from my mouth and hands on her instead of the temperature.

She was nothing like the women I normally dated, slept with, or had my arm around at events like this. I usually went for full-bodied, dark-haired women, and Gemma was the complete opposite. She had blonde hair naturally streaked with bronze, hazel eyes flecked with browns and greens, and small curves she'd hid well in T-shirts but were now on display.

As I turned away and headed toward the mansion, she whispered to herself softly. Words she didn't think I could hear but returned the grin to my face. "Idiot. You're an idiot, Gemma Hatley."

I was unspeakably pleased to find her fighting her attraction to me because she'd never once shown it during filming. She'd hardly acknowledged my existence, just like at the theater tonight. I was curious to know if it was a defense mechanism, or if there were other reasons she was resisting. Like my reputation as a Hollywood player who burned through women as fast as he changed roles. It was a mix of truth and fabrication because, for a long time, there'd only been one woman in my life. Thoughts of Mariah didn't bring me to my knees anymore, but the remnants of the pain remained even though it was more wounded ego than actual hurt.

As we entered the house, Gemma and Etta split off, winding their way deeper into Wilson's mansion packed with people in sparkling apparel and painted-on smiles. I ignored the crowd and the twinkling views from the mammoth windows set in a sea of marble and glass as I quickly found my way to the bar. I needed something to fill the ache left behind by Gemma's touch and the memories she'd unburied.

Once I had my brandy in hand, I turned to find myself surrounded by a slew of industry people—actors, actresses, directors, producers. They clamored to congratulate me, asking what I was working on even though anyone who was anyone already knew. The entire time, my eyes kept straying to Gemma. Her slinky black dress made me want to remove the thin straps with my teeth, push aside the hem, and explore with fingers and tongue what lay beyond the neon-pink panties I'd got a peek of in the car.

She made her way out the French doors to the terrace, and I yearned to go after her but forced my attention back to the auburn-haired, blue-eyed woman in front of me. Felicity Bradshaw was my costar in *Breakfast and Other Things*, and even though filming hadn't started yet, I was already tired of her. Maybe because I knew what she wanted, which was my name tied to hers not only for the benefit of the movie but because it would elevate her from the B-list she resided on. It made that dull ache of my past twist uncomfortably in my chest. I wasn't going to be anyone's fucking stepping stone again.

As gracefully as I could, I disengaged from Felicity and let my feet find their way outside. Gemma was leaning on the rail drenched in moonlight and staring out at the city lights sparkling below her. The breeze had picked up, and it sent tendrils of hair that had escaped her updo flying around her.

My body reacted to the stunning image she made, and it took almost a full minute for me to control myself enough to ease over to her. I propped my arms on the rail, and our elbows touched, sending an unexpected wave of heat spiraling through me.

"Ben Winters isn't going to win Best Actor," I said, breaking the quiet.

She looked up at me, eyes flashing, before she scooted her arm a little farther away. Her thick lashes blinked slowly, eyes darting to my lips and back.

Then, her eyes crinkled at the corners as she smiled softly. "I didn't expect you to be so thin-skinned."

"I'm not," I told her. "Just stating a fact."

She laughed, and the soft sound flew through my veins.

"God, you really do have an enormous ego," she said, smile growing.

"It isn't the only thing that's enormous." I winked at her.

She rolled her eyes, ignoring the innuendo and launching into a whole string of reasons why Ben was a contender. It wasn't just his acting, she claimed. It was the script and the timing of the movie in the industry. Every comment she made was surprisingly insightful—smart and well thought out. We bantered back and forth a bit, me adding a few things I liked about Ben's movie but also sharing what I thought the film lacked.

The debate made her come alive, and soon, she was waving her hands and speaking with a passion that enthralled me, drawing me nearer until our faces were mere millimeters apart. Her eyes were alight, and her lips were curved upward as if the discussion was making her happy, and that simple idea rocked me to the core—the thought of her being happy with me.

I lifted a finger and touched the corner of her mouth. Her smile disappeared behind a tiny gasp as my thumb skated along her bottom lip. Lust and something deeper, a primal urge to make her mine, roared through me.

"These have been tantalizing me for weeks," I

said as my finger came to rest in the middle of her mouth.

Her breath came faster, and her eyes returned my heated gaze, but instead of giving in to the feelings, she pushed my hand away. She turned back to the view of the valley spread below us, and a shiver went through her like it had when she'd stepped out of the limo.

"You're cold," I said, shrugging out of my tuxedo jacket and placing it around her shoulders.

She froze, looking at me from under lusciously long lashes. "What are you doing?"

"Being a gentleman," I told her, but the truth was, I didn't want to be a gentleman. I wanted to lead her into the guesthouse at the back of Wilson's estate, where I was staying, and devour her while the party raged around us.

She shook her head slightly. "No...what are you doing out here with me? Flirting. Making a play. I'm hardly your type, and I'm definitely not one to have a one-night fling with a celebrity just to say I did it."

The thought of having just one night with her twisted the same ridiculous primal feeling inside me. As if I knew, with an unheard-of certainty, that a few hours with her wasn't ever going to be enough.

I tucked her hair gently behind her ear.

"You don't seem like a one-night kind of woman, Gemma," I replied.

"I'm serious...Rex," she said, swallowing hard, as if saying my name was painful and beautiful all at the same time. "You need to go find someone else to hunt down. I don't want to be your prey."

I heard her no, and it filled me with regret. I wasn't like any of the assholes in my industry who'd force themselves. No meant no, regardless of the words used to express it, and she'd just told me to take a hike. Normally, I would have swiveled on my foot and taken off, but the sorrow her words brought me was so severe I couldn't leave. Not yet.

"I'm not hunting, Gemma. I've been drawn to you for weeks as if there's an invisible string tied around me, yanking me toward you. I think you're the huntress."

She closed her eyes briefly before opening them back up. "Don't throw lines like that at me."

I gave a small shrug, and my lips curled upward. "In the short time I've known you, you seem like someone who always speaks the truth. You did it with Wilson back in Tennessee. You did it tonight when it would have been easier to just agree that I'd win an Oscar. I appreciate that honesty. I like it. I like you. I'm not throwing lines. I'm giving you the truth right back."

She shook her head disbelievingly. "Is this payback, then? For me saying Ben was going to beat you? As if you have to prove to me you can act by convincing me you're into me?"

"I'm not acting with you. I *am* into you," I said and hated the stupidity of the words. Like I was thirteen and asking my first girlfriend out.

She still didn't believe me, and I knew I'd have to convince her. I put one hand on her waist, the other turning her chin to face me. My skin tingled and zapped. "I'd like to kiss you. I want to know if the insatiable need I felt by merely holding your hand was an anomaly or if it's everything I've been missing in my life."

She bit her lip again, but she didn't push me away. I risked pressing further, saying, "If after I kiss you, you want to throw my jacket at me and walk away, I'll let you and never bring it up again."

Our gazes locked, each of us searching the other for our inner truths. She seemed as wary as I was wounded. Maybe together we could find a place in the middle to actually be happy.

"One kiss," I promised.

She didn't protest, and I bent my head, gently placing our mouths together. A feathery touch that was not nearly enough, but I was determined to take it slow so I didn't scare her away. Her eyes closed, her cheeks flushed, and her hands circled my neck. When the soft tip of her tongue darted against my lips, it broke my tightly-held control, and I thrust into her mouth with a growl. She tasted like fucking heaven—sweet and mysterious. Her nails dug into my skin as I took command, licking, biting, taking what she gave and making it mine.

She moaned, and her body fell completely against me. The flames that had been brewing in my veins burst into an inferno. I tangled my hand into her hair, tugging until her head fell back, exposing her neck and allowing me to trail wet kisses down the silky length, licking the small hollow at the base before continuing downward. When I hit the silk pooling between her breasts, I slid my tongue underneath, finding her bare, and my already stiff dick grew impossibly harder. I sucked her nipple before biting softly, and she whimpered.

Suddenly, she pushed me away, and I felt the loss like a knife to my gut. She was flushed and panting as she adjusted the dress's neckline to ensure she was covered. Her eyes flashed to the French doors and the crowded room beyond them, but no one was paying us any attention. They were too busy mingling, networking, conniving to be the next big thing.

"Gemma," I said softly, grabbing her hand and twining her fingers with mine. "Don't run. Stay."

She swallowed hard, eyes traveling down my body, widening at the way my pants tented and then journeying back up. She was fighting some internal war between wanting me and needing to flee. Her jaw was clenched tightly, but her eyes were full of desire.

"I'm probably going to regret this," she said quietly.

My heart leaped, my dick rejoiced, and my arms pulled her back toward me, tasting her sweet lips again for a brief moment. Then, I turned and led her down the stairs at the side of the terrace, along the brick walk shrouded in shadows, and into the guesthouse.

As I closed the door and turned to take her in, hesitancy hit her eyes again. Caution that I needed to remove before I went further. The last thing I wanted was for her to regret this. I wanted her to ache for a repeat performance.

My hand slid along her collar bone, and her body quivered.

"Let me make love to you, Gemma."

I trailed kisses along her chest before slowly

drawing the thin strap of the dress down with my teeth just like I'd imagined. I pushed the silky material over the small slope of her breast, kissing the swell before lavishing the tip with my tongue.

"Holy hell…" she whimpered, hand going to my hair and tugging.

"Say it," I growled. "Say I can make love to you. Say I can make you quiver until you scream my name."

She nodded.

"Say the words, Gemma."

"Yes, Rex. Make love to me."

"Fuck." Those simple words made me want to explode without ever having been inside her. I picked her up, strode toward the bedroom, kicked the door shut behind us, and set her down on my bed before falling to my knees in front of her. The hem of that damn dress had been teasing me for hours.

"If there's anything I need to punish you for tonight, it's your pink panties."

Her eyes darkened, and I did exactly what I'd wanted to do since she slid inside the limo. I pulled the pink silk aside and put my mouth on her. She trembled at the simple touch, and it took only a few long, slow strokes of fingers and tongue before she was shaking, tightening, and crying out as her body shook.

She was so responsive. So perfectly glorious.

I removed the dress, her underwear, and her sexy sandals, touching, licking, and kissing every single spot I exposed. She pulled at the buttons on my vest, hands frantic, and I chuckled at her sudden impatience before stepping away to shed my layers and grab a condom from my bag. When I returned to her, she slid her fingers along my stomach, causing the muscles to flex under her touch. Gentle fingers traveled downward until she'd taken my length into her palm. I hissed at the touch, the control I prided myself on, slipping away.

I swept her into my arms, moving us further up the bed so I could explore her slowly. My lips and hands taunted and teased, savoring how her body responded to my touch, and when I finally entered her, we both gasped. Waves of unexpected emotions swam through me, an overwhelming sense of having found a rare treasure. Something I'd never want to lose.

Then, we were moving, bodies finding a rhythm that was beautiful and bold. Slow and fast, the pressure growing, the crest just beyond. I held on to my control by a hair, determined to feel her clench around me, and when she did, crying out my name in a beautiful whisper, I fell over the edge in wave upon glorious wave.

Chapter Three
Gemma

MESSAGE IN A BOTTLE
Performed by Taylor Swift

I had an unusually heavy weight on my waist and legs. Even when Etta's twenty-pound cat sat on me, it never felt like this. My brain slowly came back to life. Rex. The balcony. His lips. His hands. His body.

Shit, shit, shit!

I'd slept with Rex Carter! My hand came to my forehead. What the hell had I been thinking? I obviously hadn't been thinking. I'd stupidly given in to my body's demands. He'd felt too good with his well-practiced fingers and tongue, moves that were nothing like my one and only boyfriend's. I'd come apart multiple times last night under Rex's expert touch. My face flushed, recalling the way I'd writhed and screamed his name.

I was a moron. A cliché. I'd succumbed to a famous movie star and become another notch on his belt. At least I was a nobody, and it wouldn't be spread all over the gossip rags as it would have been if he'd hooked up with Felicity Bradshaw last night.

Still, panic filled me. It wasn't because I'd had my first one-night stand. There was nothing wrong with that. This panic was because it hadn't felt like just sex. Rex had plowed me with as many sweet words as he had gentle touches. His eyes had whispered things to me that my shielded heart had found difficult to resist, silent words that spoke of adoration and belonging.

My chest tightened. I couldn't breathe. I felt trapped underneath his weight. I pushed him off, rolled to the edge of the bed, and started to stand just as he snagged me around the waist with a muscled arm. He pulled me back against his naked chest.

"Where are you going?" he asked, face buried in my neck. The heat of his breath coasted over me, causing my nipples to harden and my core to clench. God, I'd just had sex with him mere hours ago, and my body was already greedy to repeat the experience.

This was why sleeping with him had been a mistake.

"I need to go home," I told him, but my voice was breathless, choked on emotions.

In one smooth move, he flipped us so he was on top, pinning me with his legs and his gaze. His brows furrowed together as he asked, "Why?"

"Why do I need to go home? So I can shower. So Etta doesn't think I died. So I can do the million things on my to-do list before Wilson fires me."

His fingers trailed over me, and I panted. It was ridiculous. Every single time he touched me, it felt like he was leaving a brand. A mark I'd never be able to remove no matter how many showers I took.

"First, I have a shower here. Second, you texted Etta last night if I remember right, although I was drunk on you, so maybe that part is a bit hazy. And three, it's Saturday, so you shouldn't be working."

His blue eyes were deadly serious.

"That's not how things go with Wilson, and you know it. I work seven days a week most of the time," I said. There was not an ounce of annoyance in my voice, because it didn't bother me. I loved my job. I loved this industry. The hours were long, and sometimes when I came home too tired to work on my screenplay, I wished I had a few extra minutes in a day, but that was it.

"I'm not ready to let you walk out my door yet," he grunted.

My hand brushed at his dark hair as I tried to calm the hammering in my chest.

"This isn't your door. It's Wilson's," I reminded him.

His lips twitched. "Technically, but I'm staying here while I'm filming *Breakfast and Other Things*."

I sighed internally. *Shit on toast.* Now, every time I came by the house for Wilson, I'd see him and know he was thinking of how he'd seen me naked. And I could guarantee he wouldn't be dwelling on how perfect we'd been for a handful of hours.

He watched as if he could read the way my brain was spiraling. Then, he lowered his lips and kissed me softly—almost tenderly, reverently.

"Gemma," he said, and my entire being leaped at my name on his lips. "Last night. It wasn't a one-time thing. I don't want you to leave right now. I want to spend the day getting to know you. I want to kiss you goodbye only when we're forced to go to our jobs on Monday, and then I want to find you in my bed again when I come home."

"Wh-what?"

He chuckled, and the gorgeous smile that had mesmerized me and millions of other people took over his face.

"I'm not proposing—even though it sounded like it. I'm just saying, I want to see where this goes. Us. This fucking fire. The connectedness I feel to you. I don't want you to walk out the door, thinking to yourself, *That was a nice little check off my bucket list.*"

It made my lips twitch. "Because having sex with Rex Carter was on my bucket list?"

He grinned. "Isn't it on everyone's?"

"Your ego is much, much bigger than your other body parts."

His smile went away, eyes filling in with a heat that caused a matching flame to curl through me. "I think that was a challenge."

"I've already seen it, so it's too late to challenge me."

"Then, I'll have to remind you just how enormous it is."

And he did. Making me forget everything and anything I was supposed to do that day. Making me think only of him, his hands, his body, and the way I felt like I'd found something I was missing when he was embedded inside me.

♫ ♫ ♫

My life turned into some weird montage of a romantic comedy. Every morning, I kissed Rex goodbye and promised myself I was going to spend the night at Etta's. But then, at the end of the day, he'd find me wherever I was and convince me with a single touch to go with him. Even though he was in the middle of filming and co-producing *Breakfast and Other Things*, when he was with me, his focus was completely and wholly on me. It was startling and addicting. He was breaking apart the shield I'd held over my heart since Laird had brutalized it four years ago. I knew this wasn't going to end well, but I couldn't seem to stop myself.

Just before his film was scheduled to break for Thanksgiving, Felicity showed up at the guesthouse. Her eyes widened when she saw me tucked into a corner of the couch with our wine glasses and leftover takeout boxes spread along the coffee table.

"I didn't realize you had company," she said, eyes narrowing on me, but the look she turned to Rex was all honeyed sweetness. "I wanted to work on the scene for tomorrow."

"You should have called. As you can see, I'm busy," Rex said, the disapproval clear in his tone.

She looked angry and embarrassed for all of two seconds before she hid it behind a fake smile. "Right. Sorry. What was I thinking? Of course the infamous Rex Carter wouldn't be alone."

She winked and laughed as if I was just some random hook-up, and I saw Rex's jaw clench. He'd told me he disliked working with her because she reminded him too much of the person who'd broken his heart. Mariah Temple had been his girlfriend for five years. They'd been at Yale together and had come to Hollywood together. Then, she'd used him to get a part on the film he'd been cast in and slept with the director to get an even bigger part before moving on to the president of the studio.

Felicity trailed a hand over his shoulder, regardless of me being there. Regardless of his stiff posture. "Have fun, be safe, and make sure she signs a non-disclosure agreement."

My stomach twisted with anger and regret at her words, but Rex's only response was the door clicking shut behind her. When he came back to the couch, he pulled me into his arms, buried his face in my neck, and said, "Tell me why you're here."

I hated that she'd broken open his insecurities. The ones you'd never expect the world-famous actor to have. He wanted to be loved because of who he really was, for all the things no one but those closest to him knew. Like how he had an almost genius-level IQ, a wicked sense of humor, and loved his family fiercely. Or how he was still a boy at heart, amazed by the success he'd found and terrified he'd never find someone to love him for more than his name.

My stomach turned, thinking of the screenplay I believed in with all my heart and the queries I'd been sending out for months. I hadn't told him about it because I didn't want him to think I was like Mariah...or Felicity. It made me sad that I couldn't share this piece of myself with him, but I also knew I couldn't tell him the truth. Not yet. Not until I found someone interested enough to option it without ever using his name to do so.

"Tell me," he repeated his demand, hands tightening on my waist.

I let my hand wander down to the waistband of his sweats. "I'd love to tell you it's for your looks or your stunning personality, Superstar, but it's really only one thing."

I gripped his length, and he twitched in my palm, a slow grin appearing on his face. "Yeah?"

"Yep. This *enormous* body part you still claim is bigger than your ego."

"I'm damn sure I've proven this fact to you by now."

"Maybe you need to prove it to me again."

Then, I took off at a dead run for the bedroom, and he followed me.

Chapter Four
Rex

GREAT ONES
Performed by Maren Morris

November slipped into December with Gemma and I tangled together. My days on set blended into nights locked in her embrace. She'd practically moved into the guesthouse at Wilson's with me. Her clothes were in the closet and the hamper. She had a toothbrush and makeup scattered across the bathroom counter. She was surprisingly messy for someone who prided herself on her organization in her job.

I kept her away from the set and the hungry eyes of the paparazzi as much as possible because I wanted her all to myself. But I didn't hide her from my family. When I went home for Thanksgiving, I brought her with me. My mom, dad, and my dad's boyfriend all fell head over heels for her, just like I had. She was down-to-earth, honest, and kind. I felt relaxed and at home with her.

Her family had missed her at Thanksgiving, so we went to them for Christmas. It snowed in Tennessee while we were there, and we did simple things I hadn't done since I was little, like building snowmen in the yard, sliding down the hill to the lake, and skating on the frozen water. It felt like we were making a real-life movie.

On Christmas morning, I woke up tangled with

her in the full-sized bed in her childhood room and stared down at her while she slept. I was slightly in awe of how essential she'd become to me. At how hungry I remained, not just for her body but for her smart mouth and beautiful soul.

Gemma's eyelashes fluttered open.

"Merry Christmas," she said, a soft smile lighting up her face.

"Merry Christmas, Gemma," I said, kissing her and sliding a hand under my T-shirt she'd pulled on after we'd made love last night.

She pushed my hand away. "None of that this morning. I'm surprised Sadie hasn't already pounded on the door, demanding we come down to open presents."

Gemma's sister was, impossibly, even more upbeat than Gemma herself.

I reached over to the bedside table where I'd stuck her gift in the drawer. I wanted her to unwrap it where I could see it on her naked body, glimmering and shimmering. Gemma's smile was almost shy when I handed it to her.

She moved to sit cross-legged, still close enough to me that her feet tickled my chest. "You want me to open it now?"

I nodded, my palm going to her ankle and running along her calf. I barely held back from tugging her down and devouring her. Next Christmas, we were going to have our own place so no one could demand our presence until we were ready to come out of our cocoon. My heart stuttered over that thought—the future I saw with her.

She peered into the bag and brought out a black velvet box. It was small, but not ring-sized. When she opened it, she stared for a moment before looking at me with watery eyes.

"What? How?"

"I know a guy," I said softly.

I sat up, pulled the necklace from the box, and hooked it around her neck. She twirled the charm in her fingers. It was a perfect, miniature replica of the tiara she'd brought to the set of *Wild River*. Her shit-eating grin that day had stunned me into silence, captivating me months before I'd ever touched her.

I tugged at my T-shirt, pulling it up and over her head until the necklace was sitting exactly where I wanted it—above her bare breasts, gleaming in the soft light filtering in from the window. Her blonde hair was glowing almost as much as the yellow diamond.

Her hand wrapped completely around the charm. "Thank you. It's beautiful."

"I wanted you to always remember our beginning."

She laughed. "We did not get together then. It was nine months before the premiere."

I tilted my head. "I don't think you realize, love, how much of an impact you made on me. I wanted you from the moment I saw you. But the day you walked in with this"—I tapped the replica of the tiara—"you blew my life apart."

She blushed, looking away and fidgeting. "When Laird broke my heart, Mama told me that love would find me again. That I'd know it was the forever kind of love because it would feel as if I couldn't breathe without the person next to me. That it would feel like my veins were being ripped from my body one by one. When I'm with you—"

I kissed her. Hard and fast. Demanding. It wasn't just because I hated when she talked about Laird, the man who'd promised her a future and then left her without a place to live just as she was set to start college. It was also because of the love I hadn't let her speak but that we both showed in every word and touch. Because being without her felt exactly like she'd said—as if pieces of me were being ripped away and I never got them back until our bodies and souls were touching.

A loud bang on the door was followed by Sadie's voice. "Gems, stop screwing your famous actor boyfriend and come open presents."

I grumbled, resting my forehead on her chest, and Gemma laughed. The sound filled my heart, and I sent a silent thanks out into the universe because the asshole Laird had done me a fucking favor. He'd given her up so she could become mine.

Chapter Five
Gemma

SPACE
Performed by Maren Morris

Before he'd headed to Vale with his husband, Wilson had demanded that Etta and I stay away from the office until after New Year's. He'd made us promise to have a true holiday. It left me with time to work on my script for the first time in months, and I was slightly giddy about tweaking it more. I'd received another dozen rejection notes, but I wasn't giving up.

"I want you to come to the set with me today," Rex said as he came into the living room. I panicked, sliding the printed pages into my bag before flipping around to face him with my heart beating at a wild pace that had nothing to do with my body's reaction to him.

"What's wrong?" he asked immediately with a frown.

"What? Nothing. Why do you want me to come with you?" I asked. He'd never asked me to go with him to the studio before.

"It can't be because I simply want you there?" He eased up next to me, finger sliding down my cheek while his other hand drew me closer. "I just spent twenty-four hours a day with you for five days. I'm not ready to be apart yet."

It was sweet and beautiful. He made me feel adored. Special. Cared for. He'd taken the last piece of my heart and claimed it as his own.

"I love you," I said and then covered my mouth. The words had just slipped out. I hadn't thought them through. I hadn't considered if saying them was wise. They'd just burst from me.

He smiled his fucking Rex Carter smile that made people around the world swoon before kissing me fiercely, his mouth demanding and brutal as deep emotions flew between us. Passion, love, hope. Our bodies realigned, finding a home, blending perfectly. Time seemed to stand still while we held each other until he finally pulled away with a reluctant groan.

"You're making it damn hard to be on time, but I can't growl at the others for their lack of punctuality if I'm late, too," he said, a smug smile returning to his face.

I nodded, slipped my hand into his, and said, "Let's go, Superstar."

♫ ♫ ♫

Being on the set of *Breakfast and Other Things* was nothing like being on the set of *Wild River*. Wilson had made everyone feel like family, but here, it felt as if everyone was competing. I watched as Rex single-handedly tried to bring the cast and crew together, but neither the director nor Felicity seemed to care.

Maybe it was Rex's dislike of Felicity that had vicious circles of hate burning in my chest, but watching them together, seeing her flirt and kiss him , only added to my fervent dislike. While Rex was only doing what the script called for, she continued the act long after the cameras had stopped. She was trying to make him hers. In order to distract myself, and knowing he was safely filming far away from me, I dug out my screenplay, my red pen, and my highlighter, and lost myself in it so I wouldn't be tempted to break her nose.

It wasn't until too late that I realized the director had called a break. He and Rex were in deep discussion, but Felicity had found me. She grabbed the pages from my hand before I could shove them into my bag.

"What the hell?" I growled, reaching to take them back.

I'm not sure if it was the anger in my tone or our tussle over the pages that caught Rex's attention, but he strode toward us with fury on his face. Felicity shot me a smug, knowing look as she asked, "So, is this the screenplay you've been peddling all across town?"

My heart stopped, stomach plummeting. I risked a glance at Rex. He frowned, eyes growing dark, feet stalling.

"I can see why it was rejected. No one films in black and white anymore. Who would want to? It's ridiculous," she said with a scoff. "Didn't you tell her, Rex?"

I saw Rex stiffen, and his eyes shuttered. "What?" he asked.

"Rex definitely wouldn't want his name tied to it, honey," Felicity said. "Maybe he just doesn't want to break it to you while he's screwing you."

I wasn't listening to her. I was watching Rex as he processed her words.

"You're writing a screenplay?" he asked, his tone low. "Since when?"

I bit my lip, and his gaze flicked to it and then back to my eyes.

"Since forever," I told him.

He turned and headed toward the door, and I raced after him.

"Rex, it isn't what you think," I told him.

He glanced over at me with cold eyes. "You have no idea what I'm thinking."

I scoffed, and he glared, crossing his arms over his chest.

"You think I'm using you," I said. "Your name. And I'm not."

"I should have known better," he said. "After all, you used Etta to get a job with Wilson, right? Why would I think things would be different with me?"

It was ridiculous. He knew better than that. He knew I loved him. The way we felt when we were together…it was two souls who'd been bound together for an eternity finally finding each other again in this iteration of our lives.

"I didn't use Etta," I gritted my teeth. "Yes, I wanted a job with Wilson. Yes, I accepted his offer, but I never used anyone to get it."

"You're sleeping on her couch, right? Do you even pay rent? Oh, but wait, you've found a better place to sleep these days, right? You traded up. I guess you couldn't fuck Etta into getting you a deal."

Tears sprung to my eyes at his cruel words. Ones so unlike the Rex I knew. The real Rex. The one who loved his stupid cat and his beautiful mom. The one who ached for someone to see who he was beyond the wall of fame that surrounded him.

"I understand you're hurt, but this is exactly why I didn't tell you. I was waiting until I found someone to option it. I wanted to do it on my own."

"I'm not hurt, Gemma. I'm pissed, but not at you. At myself. I knew better."

"You knew better than what?" I asked, my blood pounding so hard I thought I might pass out. My breathing was rough, almost gasping, as if I'd run five miles.

"Knew better than to believe your love came without strings."

Pain sliced through me at his words. I hated that I wasn't quick enough on my feet to have an adequate, stinging response. I hated the tears running down my face in front of the cast and crew. I hated that this would spread like wildfire through the community. I'd be lucky if my name wasn't blacklisted.

I turned on my heel and headed for the chair I'd been sitting in. Felicity was standing beside it, her expression all feline-like satisfaction. I ripped the last pages of my screenplay from her hands and shoved everything inside my bag.

She leaned in and whispered, "You were naïve if you thought you could keep him."

Then, she flounced away, her voice sickly sweet. "Rex, darling. I'm so sorry. I had no idea you didn't know she'd been throwing your name all over town."

Red-hot fury coursed through me at her lie. But I couldn't stay to fight the words. Instead, I fled from the studio with tears pouring down my face.

The next day, a car showed up at Etta's with every single belonging I'd left at the guesthouse in the backseat. I texted Rex, asking if we could talk. There was no reply.

Instead, I had a gaping wound in my soul where my heart had been because I'd given him every last piece of it. But I also realized the truth. He couldn't have truly loved me, because if he had, he wouldn't have walked away without giving me a chance to explain. He would have trusted me enough to know I'd never use him as Mariah had.

Chapter Six
Rex

BACK TO DECEMBER
Performed by Taylor Swift

Everything was cold. Gray. Lifeless.

Maybe Gemma's deception hurt worse because I'd opened up to her about Mariah. Maybe because I'd thought she'd seen the Rex Carter who existed beyond the actor label.

She'd told me she loved me.

But then, so had Mariah.

What she'd left behind was a bloodied heart that I would never let out of my chest again.

♫ ♫ ♫

Once Gemma was gone, Felicity came at me with the force of a wrecking ball, flirting and showering me with praise, telling me she could make me forget all about Gemma. But the last thing I wanted was Felicity. I still wanted what I'd had with a certain blonde-haired beauty. I wanted a sense of peace. Home. Belonging.

Because Felicity was always hanging on me, it allowed the paparazzi to spin a story that wasn't true. They turned us into the age-old tale of two actors falling in love as they filmed their rom-com. It was good publicity, and as the co-producer, I knew it for the benefit it was, but I cringed every time an image of the two of us showed up. I wondered what Gemma thought of it, and then I hardened my heart. It didn't matter.

One day, near the end of filming, Etta found me on the balcony at Wilson's. Her face was full of disgust. "Do you have to throw it in her face?"

"Excuse me?"

"You and Felicity. Gemma barely goes a night without crying herself to sleep, and you're out there fucking the person who destroyed her. You tossed aside the best thing in your life for nothing. For an argument. For something you *thought* was true but wasn't," she growled and then grimaced. "Never mind. She'd hate me for saying anything. But just so you know, she's working her ass off at two jobs now, trying to save enough money to move out so she's not *using* me, too."

For the first time since the incident on set, doubt filtered into my brain. I'd been cruel. I'd said things I hadn't meant, striking out like a wounded animal.

When I didn't respond, Etta stomped away.

I ran a hand through my hair, thinking of the first time I'd kissed Gemma in that exact spot. I'd had to basically beg her to let me do it just like I'd had to practically beg her to stay the next morning. I'd been the one to take our relationship further every time she'd tried to back away. I'd insisted she come home with me at Thanksgiving and invited myself to Christmas with her family.

Fuck.

I closed my eyes and wished I could go back to December and do everything all over again.

Chapter Seven
Gemma

MR. PERFECTLY FINE
Performed by Taylor Swift

The people filling the seats were resplendent. Perfectly coifed. Perfectly jeweled. Encased in designer brands from head to toe while I had on Keds, black jeans, and a black T-shirt with a headset that was buzzing as I raced up the back steps of the stage with the next envelope.

The awards show was only halfway through. We had a couple of hours left to go, but this was the moment I'd been simultaneously dreading and hoping for because *he* was going to be near me again.

I hated myself for the pitter-patter of my heart. I hated the way my pulse was banging so hard I thought my wrists might burst open from the pressure. I hated that I'd made sure my long blonde hair was down in the waves he'd loved to tangle his hand in as we'd come apart in his bed.

My fingers tightened on the envelope I was supposed to give him so he and *she* could announce the nominees and the winner in the Best Supporting Actress category. A twinge of bitter pleasure soared through me because at least I knew she'd never be good enough to be nominated, even if he was a shoo-in for Best Actor.

Before I could prepare myself more, he was there, stepping into the space with me. The dim lighting backstage couldn't stop him from glowing. Glimmering and shimmering from the top of his smooth, dark hair all the way down to the shiny black shoes that cost more than both my monthly salaries.

This was how we'd looked that first night—with him in a tux and me all in black. Sure, I'd had on a dress that barely covered my butt cheeks, but it had still been black. He'd spent that evening wooing me like I was somebody. Like I was going to be his next female co-star. Like I was the stars and moon, and he was simply there to adore them.

Two months. We'd had two glorious months together.

And then everything had fallen apart. I wondered how long I'd been out of his life before he'd slipped into her bed. I couldn't blame him. She was all diamond-studded belly-button rings and Prada bags to my no holes and Kate Spade knockoffs. She was first class to my coach. I was the girl from Tennessee who passed coffee to the director, and she was the next "it" girl.

Walking up to the curtain, his eyes met mine, growing just a hair because he was surprised to see me. Then, he smiled. It wasn't his real smile. I knew the real one because I'd seen it when he'd had pieces of him inside pieces of me. Parts I'd never get back.

"Gemma," his voice lowered a notch, down to the gravelly tone that made me feel like I was going to spontaneously combust. I couldn't show him how he still affected me. I wasn't an actor, but I'd learned a thing or two since he'd seen me last.

"You can't crack the envelope until you get the green light," I said, ignoring his semi-greeting and giving him the sealed parchment. Our hands brushed, and I shivered.

"How are you?" he asked, and I wanted to believe he actually cared about the answer. But before I could respond, she was there, too, wearing a dress that reminded me of mermaid tails. Blues and shimmering pink sequins that made her perfect baby-blue eyes pop out and her auburn hair shine. The camera was going to love her.

She slid her arm around his waist, leaned in, and placed a soft kiss on his cheek. Not enough to smudge her lips or leave a lipstick stain on him.

Someday, I'd have someone's arm around my waist like hers was around his. Someday, I'd look back and the wound he'd left inside me wouldn't ache like an infection. Maybe someday, I'd regrow a heart, and I'd be able to tell Mr. Perfectly Fine that I was Ms. Perfectly Okay.

Unfortunately, today wasn't that day.

"Last chance to change your mind about our bet," she whispered, her voice almost as husky as his. Sexy. Phone-operator kind of sexy.

He glanced from me to her, and he gave her the same fake smile he'd just given me.

"I'm not taking your bet, Felicity." Irritation was rampant in his tone.

She pouted, and he rolled his eyes, pulling away from her slightly.

It was stupid how my heart rejoiced, knowing he was tiring of her just as quickly as he'd tired of me.

But she wasn't going to be as easy to shake as I'd been. Their breakup would be in the press, whereas no one had known or cared when he'd walked away from me, even if I'd been worried it would hit the celebrity tabloids.

The loud applause of the audience announced the last winner leaving the stage.

"You're up," I said.

Felicity headed out the curtain without a glance in my direction, but Rex hesitated, stalling for all of two seconds as his gaze took in my hair curling well past my breasts before landing on my necklace. It was the one he'd given me for Christmas. He started to say something, but a hiss in my ear told me the cameras were already searching for him.

"Don't miss your cue," I said, turning away with my pulse leaping wildly.

I heard his shoes on the waxed floor. Heard the applause that greeted his appearance. Heard his deep baritone teasing Felicity using the lines they'd rehearsed just the day before when I'd been lost in the shadows. And I taunted myself with the truth: Mr. Perfectly Fine was never going to be mine again.

♫ ♫ ♫

I opened the email, read it twice, and shrieked.

Etta came running, hand on her heart, panic in her eyes. "What? What's wrong?"

I leaped out of the chair, squeezed her tight, and jumped around, moving us both in a little circle.

"He wants it! Ronan Hawk wants to make my

movie!" I shouted, happy tears filling my eyes. Relief. I'd been worried I'd been blacklisted when the rejections just kept coming.

Etta squeezed tight. "This is amazing! He's perfect because he's hungry to make a another great movie after his award-winner in order to prove he's not a one-hit wonder."

I nodded, the smile on my face so large I thought it might split my cheeks open. "He says he wants to make it for the Avalyn Film Festival."

"Holy shit! That's awesome."

I reached for my phone, ready to call everyone I loved, and I hated that Rex's face filled my mind. He would have been happy for me. If we'd been together, if he'd loved me, he would have been overjoyed that I'd finally gotten this opportunity.

My stomach twisted.

Then, I angrily pushed thoughts of him aside. I wasn't going to let him ruin this. No way. No how.

Chapter Eight
Rex

BYE BYE BABY
Performed by Taylor Swift

I holed up at my mom's house for a month after my Oscar win, hiding from the press and the hounding they were giving me about my supposed breakup with Felicity. They said I was drowning in despair, and they had that part right. But it wasn't because of Felicity. It was because I was the fucking loser who'd broken Gemma's heart a second time. I'd let my past ruin our future.

When Wilson called, I almost didn't answer, and as soon as he spoke, I was tempted to hang up.

"I thought you should hear it from someone who cares about you even when you don't deserve it," Wilson groused. He'd been overly growly with me since I'd ended things with Gemma.

"Hear what?" I asked, not sure I wanted to know.

"Gemma sold her screenplay to Ronan Hawk," Wilson said.

My brows drew together as I tried to place the name. When I couldn't, I grunted out, "Who the hell is Ronan Hawk?"

Wilson chuckled. "You know, the guy who won the grand prize at the Avalyn Film festival last year. The one whose been making those award-winning music videos for The Painted Daisies."

My mind flicked to a stunning piece of filmography that had won several awards.

"And he has the money to make Gemma's film?" I asked, protectiveness for Gemma filling me. I didn't want some asshole taking advantage of her.

"Well, he's now the President of Ravaged Storms Productions. I hear he just finished an exclusive tell-all with the Daisies about their lead singer being murdered that's going to blow the world away."

I sat in silence, slowly taking it all in before I finally had the courage to ask the one question that plagued me. "Have you read it?"

"Only after Ronan optioned it. She wouldn't even tell me what the two of you had fought about. It was Etta who told me, and only after I threatened to fire her if she didn't."

My gut twisted more. Gemma was working for an Oscar-winning director who absolutely would have read her script if she'd asked. He would have been honest if he thought it sucked balls, but he also would have told her how to make it better. And yet, she hadn't wanted to use that connection. One that would have gotten her screenplay much further than I could have.

Wilson's voice startled me out of my thoughts. "It's damn good, Rex. I would have loved to have gotten my hands on it. Film noir. Black and white but with random color thrown in. It's going to do really well on the festival circuit if he doesn't screw it up. It may even be an Oscar contender."

"Fuck," I said because now I wanted to make sure

it didn't get messed up. She deserved that after everything I'd accused her of. She deserved to have it take off and become something beautiful.

Wilson chuckled. "Want the good news?"

"There's good news?" I groused.

"They're looking for a lead actor who's willing to take a cut of the profits in order to keep the cost low."

My breath caught, my heart slowing and then picking up pace. Could I? Dare I? Would she even consider working with me after what I'd done? Usually, a screenwriter had very little say in the actual making of a movie, but things would be different if they were making it for the festival circuit.

"Now that I've given you the good news, I'll give you the bad," Wilson said. "I know Ronan. He's a narcissistic player known for shagging everything in his radius."

Double fuck.

"Give me his number."

Chapter Nine
Gemma

HOW YOU GET THE GIRL
Performed by Taylor Swift

"*Here you go,*" *the coffee cart* attendant said, handing me the last of the four drinks I'd ordered. I slid it into the last slot on the tray just as her eyes widened. I didn't pay it much mind in my hurry to get back to the production office, but as I spun around, I crashed head-on into a thick chest. One of the cups tipped, and a large hand caught it gracefully before it could hit the ground.

My heart slammed to a halt. I knew that hand. I knew that chest and those broad shoulders. I knew them better than I knew my own, even though I'd only been this close to them for a handful of weeks…days…a blip of time in the millions of seconds that made up my life.

"Gemma," the husky voice that most of America lost their pants over slid over me, curling through my stomach and pushing my stopped heart into a wild pace.

I hated that my body still reacted this way to him.

When I glanced up, his blue eyes were dark and hooded, full of emotions I couldn't afford to read, including the desire that had led me to his bed to begin with.

"Rex," I greeted and went to sidestep him, to hurry along to where Ronan was waiting for me in his office at the back of the studio lot.

But Rex's hand slipped to my wrist, halting me.

"I haven't been able to get you out of my mind. I miss you," he said, dropping his voice so only I could hear it.

Even as my weak knees trembled at the words I'd longed to hear for months, my brain and my heart hardened. I couldn't let him know he still had power over me. I made my face a blank slate, carefully pulled my hand away, and headed toward my meeting without responding.

"Gemma!" His deep voice sounded pained, and because it was louder, it drew eyes.

I still ignored it, and to my utter shock, he fell into stride alongside me, keeping pace as I hurried across the blacktop.

"I'm late. I don't have time for this," I said.

"You're going to Ronan's, right?" he asked.

I shot him a surprised look. How did he know? Then, my stomach flipped over. No! No, no, no, no, no. It couldn't be, could it? He wasn't reading for the part, was he?

When I didn't reply, he kept going. "I've signed on as the lead."

My feet forgot to walk. "What? Why?"

His gaze bore into me, trying to read my soul as he'd once done easily.

"Why wouldn't I want an amazing part in an incredibly written screenplay?" he asked, lips lifting slightly at the corner.

I snorted. "It's a tiny production that may never make it to the mainstream theaters."

"It's going to be nominated for an Oscar," he said with a confidence I didn't have. The words stabbed and tore at me while simultaneously filling me with pride that he thought my words were worthy of an award.

"There's no way Ronan can afford to pay you even a tenth of your going rate," I said instead of acknowledging the compliment.

He shrugged. "I've negotiated a cut of the profits in lieu of a salary."

I closed my eyes, trying not to let his words affect me, but it was impossible. Having a name like Rex's attached to our production would bring much-needed attention…and money. Rex knew it. He knew it and was doing it anyway. After he'd basically accused me of using him to get just this, he'd gone ahead and done it anyway—without my knowledge, acceptance, or asking. I turned away and resumed my walk toward Ronan's office.

"I was a fool, Gemma," he called, jogging slightly to catch up.

I couldn't look at him. I couldn't give the tiny pinprick of hope that those words brought to my heart a chance to grow. It had taken me months to not cry myself to sleep. I was still not over the loss. There was something wrong with me that whenever I got my heart broken, it took me years to mend. It was a character flaw, but at least I knew it. At least I'd be even more careful the next time someone tried to steal my heart.

"Say something," he demanded.

"What do you want me to say, Rex?"

"That you've missed me, too."

God, he was going to undo me. Unravel the little bit of dignity and strength I had left.

"Do you miss Felicity, also?" I asked, groaning internally, wishing I could take it back.

"I was never with Felicity!" he growled. "You should know me better than that."

I snorted. "Should I? Know you better? Because I thought you knew me well enough to know I wouldn't use you just to get a screenplay read, but obviously I was wrong."

The painful words slipped out as the barely scabbed holes inside me broke open.

"I do know you. I was just an idiot, wrapped up in my head and my past. Let me prove to you I can do better. Be better," he said with a determination written all over his face that made it hard to breathe.

I'd barely been able to resist him the first time he'd demanded anything of me. *Just a kiss*, he'd said. One kiss. And my life had imploded. My gaze fell to his lips. My body ached to be tucked up against his. I missed him. Missed his body commanding mine and his sweet words filling my heart. But the pain… God, the pain was unbearable.

Suddenly, he moved, wrapping an arm around my waist and tossing my tray to the ground. "What the h—"

He shoved his lips against mine.

Lips that talked to me as they had from the very first moment they'd touched mine six months ago. Lips that demanded a response from the very depths of me and littered my skin with goosebumps. My entire body lit up, flames leaping from my stomach, journeying along my veins, and trying to escape from my fingertips. Desire I'd never known except with Rex.

My body sagged into him. A physical response I couldn't control. When we'd touched, we'd always been a fiery inferno. One I'd been unable to deny. But he had. He'd thrown us away only days after giving me a necklace that was supposed to forever remind us of our beginning.

That thought had me yanking away from him. I brushed the back of my hand across my lips, pissed that they were shaking with need.

"Tell me you don't miss that," he growled, guttural and low, the sound only adding to the fuel in my belly. "Tell me you don't feel like you've found the missing piece of your soul when we touch, and I'll walk away."

"Again. You mean you'll walk away *again*," I said, eyes narrowing.

He put a hand to his chest.

"It was the biggest mistake of my life. I'd never felt the depths of emotions you caused to roar through me whenever we touched, and I think it terrified me as much as I loved it. And then…then when I found out about your screenplay, I convinced myself you were like the others, using me for what I could do for you."

"That's why I hid it from you!" I yelled, frustration welling through me. "It wasn't just that I didn't want you to think I was using you. I didn't want to ride on your coattails. I wanted any success I got to be my own. To prove *I* could do this."

He nodded. "I know that now. And I can't say sorry enough. All I know is that I need you."

I laughed sarcastically, and my eyes were drawn to the people around us who'd stopped to watch Rex Carter woo some unknown. There were even a few phones pointed in our direction. I rolled my eyes. Just what I needed. Publicity. People thinking the only reason my screenplay was being produced was because I was his new plaything.

"You can't do this to me!" I hissed.

Rex looked around and saw the same thing I did, but instead of being embarrassed by it, instead of pulling me into a dark corner, he did the opposite. He drew more attention by bending down on one knee as if he was going to propose—which we both knew he wasn't. He'd never propose in public like this.

It still caused me to flush a thousand shades of red, the heat of it crossing my cheeks and going down my neck.

"Gemma Hatley, I'm begging you to forgive me. To give me a second chance. To let me prove to you that the way our bodies talk when we're joined together is something special. That the way you complete my thoughts and the way I read everything you're feeling means we are supposed to be together. Let me prove that the fates weren't wrong when they thrust you into my life like a golden arrow."

I couldn't help but laugh. The ridiculousness of it. Yet the poorly formed speech threatened to unravel the strings I'd tied around my heart to hold it together after he'd broken it into pieces.

He grinned. "I'm not the writer, obviously. That's your job. Tell me what I should say instead. Tell me what words will win you back."

I closed my eyes against a sudden rush of tears. God, I'd wanted this for months. Losing him had been like having half my body ripped from me. Even though he'd been a famous star, when we'd been together, we'd felt like two regular people, sharing our lives.

And then he'd thrown it away.

He pulled my hand into his, tugging me so I ended up sitting on his knee. His free hand wiped at the tears I hadn't even realized were running down my face and then tangled in my thick mess of blonde hair.

"I'll spend the rest of my life making it up to you. I'll spend the rest of my life screaming from the mountaintops how you're the one and only woman for me if you'll give me this second chance to show you how very much I mean it."

"We're being photographed," I said, but there was a soft smile emerging on my lips. Hope rushed through me and my heart began a silent chant: *What if he means it?*

"I don't care," he said with force. His tone was deep and full of emotions.

He hated the press and the public invading his personal life. It was why we'd kept to ourselves so much, but he didn't seem the least bit concerned now.

Almost as if he wanted it. Relished it. He actually turned and waved at the woman with her phone up, trying to be sly, when we all knew it was going to be on social media the moment she stepped away.

"You broke my heart," I told him solemnly.

He nodded, the pain in his expression clear. "And every day for the rest of our lives, I promise to lace it back together. With love and devotion and kisses."

God…could I trust him? The famous actor who regularly convinced the world that what he was saying on screen was true.

"You once told me your mama said love was a living, breathing entity and that refusing it entrance into your life would be like kicking a puppy."

I snorted. "That wasn't what she or I said at all."

He grinned, hypnotizing me.

"It's the idea of it, though."

"Stick to the acting, Rex. Let others write the words."

"I'll let you write all my words for the rest of my life," he said with a sincerity I could feel in his heart as it beat wildly beneath my fingers.

"That's a long time," I said.

"It isn't long enough."

My soul was screaming at my stupid mind to stop thinking. To just trust the way our bodies felt together. To forgive a mistake that could be mended.

I pulled my hands from where they sat joined with his on his chest, and his eyes flickered with sadness. Then, I placed my palms on his cheeks, drawing his face closer to mine.

"If you hurt me again, I'll kill off every character you ever want to play."

His smile grew, and a deep laugh filled his chest.

"If I hurt you again, I'll stop acting."

It was a huge promise for an A-lister to make when he was at the top of his career.

I placed my lips on his, and I felt him sigh against them. A sigh of relief. A sigh of coming home after being gone too long. Rex gave a throaty noise, a mix of pleasure and longing, and then his tongue darted against the seam of my lips, pushing gently, parting mine, tasting me as he moved along the crevices, finding all the inner parts of me that he'd once adored and then abandoned. I hesitated before returning the movement of his tongue with my own. His arms tightened around me, forcing away any distance that had been left between us and holding me steady as he reached into me and reclaimed all the spots that had once been his.

A cough next to us brought our faces to Ronan's dancing eyes.

"I see you two have met," he laughed.

"She's my whole world," Rex responded.

Even though the words were cliché, just like so many things about Rex and me and our lives, I didn't want any others. Because Mr. Perfectly Fine had finally and truly become mine.

♫ ♫ ♫

Want to know more about Ronan Hawk and the murder that derailed his documentary? You can find out in the fast-paced series from LJ Evans. With an all-female rock band and the alpha heroes who steal their hearts, this romantic suspense series might just leave you breathless.

Check out the **THE PAINTED DAISIES** today!

If you want to catch more of Gemma, her family, and her home town of Willow Creek before she met Rex, read her brother's **full-length, single-dad, grumpy-sheriff HEA in** *THE LAST ONE YOU LOVED* on Amazon today, or keep reading for the first few chapters here.

SAMPLE
THE LAST ONE YOU LOVED

PROLOGUE
Maddox

AIN'T ALWAYS THE COWBOY

Performed by Jon Pardi

The lake shimmered in the moonlight. The warm breeze stirred up tiny waves, sending white sprinkles shifting across the surface as it drifted toward the shore where we were parked.

We were on the tailgate of my beat-up Bronco with our hands and limbs joined. McKenna's jean-clad legs were flung over my lap, and her head rested on my shoulder. Her cowboy boots were off, lost somewhere behind me in the chaos of blankets and food wrappers. I ran the fingers of my free hand over the gentle arch of her foot, and she jerked it away, laughing.

"Don't you dare tickle me unless you want to end up with a busted nose," she teased, her soft voice washing over me.

It wasn't like I hadn't known she'd pull away. Ten years of knowing her meant I knew just how ticklish her feet were, but I'd done it anyway in an attempt to lighten the mood. But the sound and scent and feel of her made it almost impossible to feel anything but sorrow. It might be the last time I would hold her like this, and my heart screamed as if it could change what was happening by merely twisting inside my chest.

"Wanna go for a swim?" I asked.

It was still humid outside, even though the sun had set hours ago. Long enough that the twilight sounds of the bugs and wild animals had almost disappeared. Instead, a quiet had taken over the space, a preview of what would happen once she drove down the road tomorrow and my life was forever changed.

In answer to my question, she slid off of me and started discarding clothes. She was wearing a string bikini under her jeans and floaty blouse, as if she'd known I'd ask for this—us in the water. I swallowed hard at the gentle curves I'd spent years getting to know as well as my own. I glanced down at my sinewy body toughened from years of working on the ranch. She'd always said my muscles were the very best kind—built from hard work. Would anyone else ever care about them the way she had?

I hadn't been as prepared as she'd been for a swim, so my boxer briefs were going to have to do. Once I'd stripped down, I recaptured her hand, determined to touch her for as long as possible, and led us toward the water, picking our way through the twigs and rocks as we went.

As soon as we hit the cool water, I shivered. It was a soothing relief to the heat and heaviness of the day. If only it could lift the weight inside me as easily as it chilled my skin.

We swam toward the makeshift dock someone had fastened to the middle of the lake decades ago. We didn't pull ourselves up on top. Instead, we hid in the shadows. She wrapped her long limbs around my waist, and I looped an arm through one of the ropes hanging off the wooden slats to hold us steady while my hands continued to touch her.

She kissed me. Wet and wild. Slow and torturous. Love and goodbyes blended into the movements as we rejoined our bodies in the way we'd been doing over the last couple of months. Like a flame on the wick of a firecracker, burning, burning, burning until it finally ignited into a shower of light and sound.

Until it became nothing but us.

She moaned into my mouth when my fingers slid under her bikini, touching pieces of her that were aching for me. I wanted to cry out as well, but with a different ache. I wanted to let my tears wash into the lake.

But it would be selfish because I wouldn't be crying for her. I'd only be crying for me, and that didn't seem fair. McKenna deserved the future she was heading toward—her dream of becoming a doctor finally starting. But her desire to escape this town and her mother hurt because it meant she was escaping me and my family as well—the people who'd loved and sheltered her.

Knowing it was coming hadn't eased the pain of its arrival. As much as I wanted to follow her, I couldn't. My life was here with my family, and the ranch, and my own dreams of serving my community. Even if everything at home had been perfectly fine, I wasn't sure I'd want to leave our small town for a place where you couldn't see the stars. Here, they were so bright it seemed like you could grab them, put them in your pocket, and take them with you. If I was forced to live in a city, I'd burn out just like those faraway suns. If you forced her to stay, she'd wither like the roses I'd given her last week. Dust into dust.

We loved each other more than I'd ever thought was possible, especially considering we were just two kids, barely legal. I knew her smiles and looks and moods better than she knew them herself, and vice versa. But this was where the road we were on finally divided after a decade of running side by side. A bitter taste rose inside me because I wasn't sure our roads would ever cross again.

"I'll come visit," I told her, breaking my mouth from hers. "Thanksgiving or spring break. Whichever works."

Could I get through to spring without seeing her? Touching her? Loving her? How would I even come up with the money for the trip?

She rested her forehead on my shoulder, placed a gentle kiss there, and then looked up at me with sad, tormented eyes.

"Maddox…between college, medical school, and a residency, it'll be at least eleven years before I'm done. I'll always be your friend. I'll always love you…but…I just…" A choked sob broke free from her, and my throat bobbed, eyes watering.

"You want to break up. You don't even want to try?" I asked, that bitterness coating my tongue and my mouth growing. She had choices. She could have applied to Tennessee State. She could have kept us closer, but even as I said it, I knew she couldn't. McKenna needed to put her childhood behind her…even if that meant giving me up along with it.

She put her hands on my cheeks, cupping them and kissing my lips sweetly.

"You're my favorite thing. My favorite memory. My favorite gift. My favorite person," she said quietly.

I could no longer hold the tears back. I didn't know how to let her go. But I'd have to because it wasn't always the cowboy who ran away.

Sometimes, it was the golden-haloed woman with

a future so bright the gods had to be jealous.

That was my McKenna.

And tomorrow, she'd be gone.

No longer mine, but the world's instead.

Chapter 1
McKenna

YOU ALL OVER ME
Performed by Taylor Swift with Maren Morris

TEN YEARS LATER

Bouncing on my bed woke me. I forced my eyes open and then slammed them shut upon seeing Sally's glowing face. It was too early for this kind of over-the-top happiness.

"Happy birthday, McKenna!" she practically screamed, forcing me to look at her again.

I groaned and tried to bury my head under the covers, but my roommate wouldn't let me. Instead, she ripped the blankets back with surprisingly strong hands and shoved a heavy present at me. Her large, mahogany eyes twinkled in her light-brown face as her pink-tipped waves swung around her sharply defined cheeks and chin.

I hated birthdays, while Sally was from a family who celebrated them like they were a bigger deal than Christmas. In the three years I'd been living with her, she'd made sure I had cake, presents, and whatever I wanted for dinner. Last year, she'd even thrown a surprise party for me at the nurses' station. I'd wanted to run as soon as I'd turned the corner, and I'd made her promise never to do it again.

Growing up, my birthdays had been a painful reminder of what had gone wrong in Mama's life, and she'd done everything to make sure her worst day would also be mine. Only one person besides Sally had ever tried to make this day something different.

I pushed aside the memories that threatened to weigh me down and groused without any real heat, "It's too early for presents and celebrations, Sal."

"Shut up and open it!" she said, ignoring my grumpiness and shoving the box at me with her wide smile fixed permanently in place.

I sat up, and my naturally blonde hair tumbled around me in knots. I'd regret going to bed with it wet, but I'd been exhausted after my twelve-hour shift at the hospital had turned into a sixteen-hour one. I'd barely been able to shower, let alone worry about my hair.

I pulled the bulky gift onto my lap and shot Sally a frown. "I hope you didn't do something stupid, like spend some of your car money on me. I don't want to be the reason you can't get it in January!"

She flicked my shoulder. "Just open it and stop being ridiculous."

I slowly undid the ribbon and pulled off the lid. Inside was a DVD collection of Buffy the Vampire Slayer. Every season. I swallowed hard. The DVDs weren't new, but they still had to have cost her a pretty penny to get the entire set. With both of us barely scraping by due to the enormous college debt resting on our shoulders, this wasn't a little gift.

Tears hit my eyes for real, but I refused to let them out, like I'd learned to do early in life by biting my cheek and clenching my nails into my palms. But my voice was still clogged with emotions when I choked out, "Dang it, Sal."

She hugged me to her, and I did my best not to stiffen, letting my head land briefly on her shoulder.

"Now, you'll always have Buffy when you need her," she said softly.

"I need her less these days because I have you," I responded. She was the best female friend I'd ever had. I'd say she was my best friend ever, but there was a teeny-tiny place inside my heart that knew it would be a lie. But I wouldn't hear from him today. I'd shoved him out of my life for a dream—a mirage—that had disappeared in the shimmer of the hot sun.

My gut twisted.

I couldn't think of that today. Of him. Of my mistakes.

I had to get my head on straight, put on my white jacket, and head to the ER—to the real dream I was mere months away from finalizing.

Once my residency was over, I'd be one-hundred-percent official. I'd not only be a doctor, but I'd also be able to call the shots. Goosebumps covered my arms. Ten-year-old me would hardly be able to believe it. That I'd actually escaped and made it happen.

"Get dressed. Your birthday breakfast awaits," Sally said and basically pushed me out of the bed. I stumbled, barely catching myself on the dresser.

"Geez, if this is how you treat a friend on her birthday, I don't want to see how you treat your enemies," I teased.

She headed for the door. "If you're not out in five minutes, I'm going to shove your pancakes—whipped cream and all—in your face. Dickwad Gregory is in charge today, so neither of us can afford to be late."

My stomach knotted thinking of the head of the ER department. He was obnoxious, and egotistical, and thought everyone should swoon over his fifty-year-old, married self. Worse, some people did. Made me pukey even thinking about it.

"McK, I'm not kidding. Five minutes," Sally said, bringing me out of my thoughts.

"Okay, okay."

I slipped into the bathroom, washed up, and pulled on my scrubs. As I fought to drag my messy hair into a high ponytail, the shadows under my hazel eyes caught my attention. They'd pretty much become a permanent feature since starting my residency and were almost as black as my heavy brows. My hand stalled as it hit me suddenly—I looked like Mama.

That scared me. My tired expression wasn't from drugs and alcohol, but it was from running fast and furious for too many years.

"McK!" Sally hollered.

I shoved my phone, water bottle, and keys into a small backpack and hurried out of the room before coming to a complete stop, mouth dropping open.

The entire apartment was full of balloons and streamers.

I bit my cheek hard, tasting blood, and blinked rapidly to hold back the waterworks. Sally was all but dancing around me, excitement on her face from the pure joy of doing this for me.

I didn't care about my birthday. But I thanked the universe for the day Sally had found me on the bench outside the hospital, in a rare fit of tears, and befriended me. It was almost as important as the day Maddox Hatley had found me cowering in a shed behind his uncle's bar when I was eight.

Too bad I didn't have Maddox anymore.

It made this, what I had with Sally, that much more important. So, I'd celebrate today because she wanted me to. Because she was literally the only soul left on this planet who would care if I disappeared tomorrow.

Chapter 2
Maddox

SLOW BURN
Performed by Zac Brown Band

I pulled back just in time, letting the fist barely graze my chin. The movement was enough to send my Stetson flying, landing amongst the straw where it was going to get trampled. It was the sight of my hat on the ground that pissed me off more than the fist or Willy Tate's drunken, angry snarl as he lunged for me again.

I ducked the second shot and shoved my shoulder into his gut, taking him down to the ground with me. The music had stopped, the customers in the bar quiet as they watched two burly men wrestle. Several chairs were tipped over, tables were bumped, and drinks were spilled as we rolled around. It took me one too many moves before I finally had him pinned facedown with his hands behind his back and my knee holding him in place.

"Damn it, Willy, you owe me a new hat!" I growled.

Clapping filled the air along with hoots and hollers that made my eyes roll.

"Thanks for the show!" someone in the back yelled as someone else shouted out, "Brings me back to my sheep-tying days!"

"Thanks for the help, y'all," I said sarcastically, eyeing my brother sitting calmly on a stool at the bar with a crooked grin.

"Why, Sheriff Maddox, no one would ever presume to think you needed help." Ryder's grin grew, and then he had the audacity to wink at me as he raised a beer in my direction. I barely resisted flipping him the bird as laughter erupted from him, causing his blue eyes that matched mine to crinkle at the corners. He brushed a hand over his perfectly tousled dark-brown hair that should have been smashed flat after wearing a hat all day but instead looked like he'd stepped off the page of a damn magazine.

I was not anywhere near picture-perfect. My dark-blond hair was standing up in places, and the stubble on my chin—a day past trendy—was dripping and sticky from the whiskey Willy had thrown at me. The alcohol had stained my tan shirt, and our scuffle had snagged the ends of my olive-green tie, almost ripping it from my neck.

"She left me, Maddox. For a goddamn suit from Knoxville." Willy was crying now, and it almost looked ridiculous on the six-foot-three mechanic with the hair and beard of someone who'd been lost in the wild for one too many years.

"Taking it out on everyone here isn't going to make the pain go away, shithead," I grumbled. "You gonna start swinging again if I get up?"

Willy shook his head. I stood and then helped the man to his feet. His sad, puppy-dog eyes were full of tears that tumbled down his cheeks.

"You going to arrest him for hitting a lawman?" Gemma asked, trying not to giggle. My sister was sitting next to Ryder at the bar. Her long hair was the same color as mine, but her hazel eyes were full of our brother's laughter. Ryder tapped her elbow with his in appreciation of the taunt she'd thrown my way.

Willy hunched his enormous shoulders. "Fuck. I forgot you're the sheriff now."

"I've been an officer of the law for damn near six years, Willy. Hitting me before or after I'd been elected wouldn't change a damn thing." I leaned down and picked up my hat, brushing it against my thigh and shoving him toward the door of McFlannigan's. It was the only bar in town and normally looked as Irish as my uncle who owned the place, but on Thursdays, they had two-dollar beers, line dancing, and a live band. Uncle Phil brought hay in from the ranch to make it more Tennessee barnyard than Dublin dive.

I'd told him more than once the hay was a hazard, but as he was friends with the county health inspector, who just happened to be in one of the booths tonight with his wife, my uncle clearly didn't have to worry about being fined. That was the way everything in this town worked, and while I'd been able to turn a blind eye to some of it as a deputy, since I'd been elected, it had been harder to do.

The people of Winter County had put their trust in me. Maybe it was because Sheriff Haskett had thrown his hat in my direction when he'd stepped down, or maybe it was because the Hatley family had been in Willow Creek since its inception. Regardless, they'd taken a chance on a green twenty-seven-year-old last year, and I'd spent twelve months proving to them it had been the right choice.

Willy and I were at the door when Ryder called out, "Going to come back and have a beer with us after you get him home?"

I shook my head.

"Come on, Maddox, one drink!" Gemma called.

I had no desire to sit at the bar, shooting the shit with my siblings, after the long day I'd had. If the bar hadn't been mere blocks from my house when the call had come in as I walked out the station door, I would've let one of my deputies handle the call. Now that I'd done my civic duty for the night, I had only one goal, and that was getting home to my girl.

I directed Willy into the passenger seat of my ancient green and rust-covered Bronco, wishing I'd driven my sheriff truck instead. But the Bronco had called to me this morning—the date dragging at me as it did every year.

The date I tried to ignore and failed miserably to do.

I got Willy tucked into the small apartment above the garage his family had owned almost as long as mine had owned the ranch and then headed to my 1950s-style bungalow two streets over. After three years of hard work, the house was pretty much how I wanted it. The wood siding had a fresh coat of pale-yellow paint, new black shutters edged the multi-paned windows, and a burnt-orange custom door invited you in, just like the swing tucked in the corner of the front porch.

An antique lamp on the hall table cast a gentle light onto the dark plank floors as I let myself in, and the murmur of the television in the open-space living area greeted me. Rianne looked up from the cushy, leather couch I'd spent a small fortune on as I hung my destroyed hat on the rack by the door.

Her bright-red lips curved upward in greeting, and her dark-brown face was just starting to show signs of wrinkles even though she was as old as my grandparents. Her black-and-white corkscrew hair was tucked beneath a vivid-blue scarf littered with pictures of baby ducks. She had so many head wraps I thought she could wear a different one every day of the year and still have more.

"How is she?" I asked.

"Like always. Pretending to sleep but really waiting for you," she said, turning off the TV and rising. She was wearing soft jeans and a long tunic top, looking far more casual than she ever had as my third-grade teacher. When I'd been a rowdy eight-year-old, I'd adored her, and now that she'd turned in her teacher badge and taken on helping me, I loved her almost as much as I loved my mama.

"You smell like a liquor cabinet." Rianne's nose squished up, but there was a smile on her lips.

I sighed, ran my hand over my half-assed, alcohol-soaked beard, and grimaced.

"Had to pull Willy out of McFlannigan's before he tore it apart."

Rianne's face fell. "Aw, he's taking the loss of his woman pretty hard."

I nodded. It was why I'd tucked him at home instead of locking him up in a cell at the station. I knew what it felt like to watch your woman drive away. The agony I'd felt didn't make me want to bleed out on the floor anymore, but the reminder on this day, more than any other, made the hurt tumble through me as if it had happened yesterday instead of a decade ago.

Rianne gathered her things, and I walked her to the door.

"Try to get some rest tomorrow, and I'll see you on Sunday," she said before leaving.

I was technically off the clock for a whole day, but that never meant much when you were one of only twelve people holding down the only law enforcement agency in the county. We didn't have a lot of crime in Willow Creek, but we did have a lot of work. On any given day, I might be helping round up stray chickens one moment and taking beer from underage kids at the lake the next. The biggest pain in my ass was the motorcycle club, The West Gears, who used their headquarters up in the mountains right at the county line to deal drugs and store stolen merchandise. The Gears were the reason I was dead on my feet tonight after a day of hunting them down.

I headed down the hall, feet stalling as I passed Mila's door. She'd expect me to crawl into bed with her, and I didn't want to do that smelling like whiskey, so I continued on to the one room I hadn't let Mama or my sisters help decorate. Instead, the main bedroom reflected me like almost no other part of the house. It was full of dark woods, navy linens, and black-and-white photographs of the lake and the ranch.

I locked my weapon away in the gun safe, showered in the bathroom filled with teak woods and blue linens, and then changed into sweats and a long-sleeve T-shirt before padding on bare feet back to Mila's room. I turned the knob as quietly as possible in a vain hope that she might actually be asleep but chuckled to myself when I saw her dart her head under the covers.

Her room looked like a rainbow had thrown up in it. She was obsessed with them. She'd even convinced me to paint her white headboard in rainbow stripes. Between that, her four pastel-colored nightlights, and the pile of stuffed unicorns that filled an armchair in the corner, it felt like walking into a cartoon world. I crossed the faux-fur white rug and stood looking down at the rainbow comforter that shed glitter like it was a cat changing seasons.

"Oh good, Mila is asleep. I don't have to read The Day the Unicorns Saved the World for the one-thousandth time," I said softly.

The covers were thrown back, and beautiful wheat-colored eyes stared at me under thick brows that were almost black and contrasted with the honey-blonde hair spiraling in waves around her round face. "I'm not sleeping, Daddy! You have to read it, or I'll be up all night."

There was a little whine to her sweet voice and a pout to her lips that made my mouth twitch. I sighed dramatically, looked up at the ceiling, and pretended to contemplate the fate of my life before pulling the book from her nightstand.

"Scootch over," I said as if this wasn't our nightly routine.

She pulled back her covers and moved to the side as I slid in with her. Her tiny, five-year-old body curled up against me, and I put one arm around her, holding her tight. She smelled like the berry shampoo Mama had bought for her birthday, and she had on a pair of fuzzy, pink-striped pajamas that had been from my sister. Her body was warm and her tiny hand soft as she placed it on my arm. My heart filled to near bursting just by having her there.

"How was your day?" I asked.

"I learned that the letter L says lllll like in lion, and that five and two more is seven. Seven is my birthday number, so Mrs. Randall let me use the butterfly pointer and lead the class in the alphabet song."

Kindergarten. My baby had started kindergarten at the end of August. I hadn't expected it to be as hard as it had been to drop her off at school and walk away. I mean, I'd been leaving her every day for the four years of her life that she'd been mine. But there was something different about leaving her with Rianne versus taking her into a classroom full of kids who I couldn't guarantee would be nice and adults who were strangers. I'd run the name of the principal and every teacher at the school to make sure there weren't any scumbags hiding in the system, even when I knew the state wouldn't have given certificates to criminals. I'd sort of gone off my rocker for a day or two. The only thing that made it easier was knowing Mila liked being there.

"That sounds like a really good day," I told her.

"Yeah. But Missy wouldn't give me a turn with the hula hoop." She pouted, and every vein in my body tightened. The need to protect her, even from other five-year-olds, was a strange sensation. There was a time in my life when I hadn't wanted to be a dad, when I'd promised another blonde-haired girl that we wouldn't have kids because she was adamantly opposed to having them.

"I'll buy you your own damn hula hoop tomorrow," I told her, voice gruff with emotions. She giggled.

"You cussed again, Daddy. You owe me another dollar for the cuss jar."

I smiled with my lips against her hair. She'd have enough money in that jar to go to college if I wasn't careful. The thought of her being grown up and going away to college threatened to rip some more at the scars that had already cracked open today.

I pushed the pain away, opened the book, and started reading as my girl snuggled deeper into my chest. My heart expanded until it was quadruple the size it should have been. This was perfect. I didn't need anything else in my life but this.

KEEP READING
THE LAST ONE YOU LOVED
TODAY
https://geni.us/TLOYL
FREE IN KINDLE UNLIMITED

Books By L J
Standalone

After All the Wreckage — Rory & Gage

A single-dad, small-town, romantic suspense

He's a broody bar owner raising his siblings. She's a scrappy PI who's loved him since she was a teenager. When his brother disappears, she forces aside years of family secrets to help him.

Charming and the Cherry Blossom — Elle & Hudson

A small-town, he-falls-first, contemporary romance

Today was a fairy tale…I inherited a fortune from a dad I never knew, and a thoroughly charming guy asked me out. But like all fairy tales, mine has a dark side...and my happily ever after may disappear with the truth.

Title TBD — Fallon & Parker – Coming Soon

A small-town, grumpy bodyguard, romantic suspense

Second chances, childhood crushes turned into adult passion, and a mystery that will keep you on your toes.

The Hatley Family Standalones

The Last One You Loved — Maddox & McKenna

A single-dad, grumpy-sheriff, romantic suspense

He's a small-town sheriff with a secret that can unravel their worlds. She's an ER resident running from a costly mistake. Coming home will only mean heartache…unless they let forgiveness heal them both.

The Last Promise You Made — Ryder & Gia

A single-dad, grumpy-cowboy, romantic suspense

He's a grumpy rancher who swore off all relationships. She's a spitfire undercover agent who brings danger to his life. Desire is an inconvenience. Falling in love is absolutely out of the question…

The Last Dance You Saved — Sadie & Rafe

A single-dad, grumpy-cowboy, romantic suspense

Sadie's world is disrupted by a grumpy cowboy who thought he'd left the ranch and relationships behind for good. When danger finds them and he tries to send her away, she proves that with love at stake, she's willing to risk it all.

Perfectly Fine — Gemma & Rex

A fish-out-of-water, celebrity romance

He's a charming, A-list actor at the top of his game. She's a determined, small-town screenwriter hoping for a deal. They form an unexpected connection until heartbreak ruins their future. Available on Amazon and also FREE eBook with newsletter subscription.

Matherton Family Standalones

Lost in the Moonlight — Lincoln & Willow

A grumpy-sunshine, small-town, romantic suspense

My new neighbor is all too enticing, but I have one job—to stay hidden—and the media's fascination with Lincoln can destroy my safe haven. So why can't I stay away?

LITD — Katerina & Axel – Coming Soon

A growly-bodyguard, single-dad, romantic suspense

LITH — Juliette's HEA – Coming soon

A single-dad, tormented-musician, romantic suspense

The Anchor Novels

Guarded Dreams — Eli & Ava

A grumpy-sunshine, forced-proximity, military romance

He's a grumpy Coast Guard focused on a life of service. She's a feisty musician searching for stardom. Nothing about them fits, and yet attraction burns when fate lands them in the same house for the summer.

Forged by Sacrifice — Mac & Georgie

A roommates-to-lovers, second-chance, military romance

He's a driven military man zeroed in on a new goal. She's a struggling law student running from her family's mistakes. Nothing about them fits until one unforgettable kiss threatens their roommate status and their plans along with it.

Avenged by Love — Truck & Jersey

A fake-marriage, forced-proximity, military romance

When a broody military man and a quiet bookstore clerk share a house, more than attraction flares. Watching her suffer in silence has him extending her the only help he can—a marriage of convenience to give her the insurance she needs.

Damaged Desires — Dani & Nash

A frenemy, bodyguard, military romance

Reeling from losing his team, a growly Navy SEAL battles an attraction for his best friend's fiery sister, until a stalker puts her in his sights. Now he'll do anything to protect her, even take her to the one place he swore he'd never go—home.

Branded by a Song — Brady & Tristan

A single-mom, small-town, rock-star romance

He's a country rock legend searching for inspiration. She's a Navy SEAL's widow determined to honor his memory. Neither believes the attraction tugging at them can lead to more until her grandmother's will twines their futures.

Tripped by Love – Cassidy & Marco

A bodyguard, single-mom, small-town romance

She's a busy single mom with a restaurant to run, and he's her brother's bodyguard with a checkered past. They're just friends until a little white lie changes everything.

The Anchor Novels: The Military Bros Box Set

The 1st three books + an exclusive novella

Guarded Dreams, Forged by Sacrifice, and *Avenged by Love* plus the novella, *The Hurricane*! Heartfelt military romance with love, sacrifice, and found families. The perfect book-boyfriend binge read.

The Anchor Suspense Novels

Unmasked Dreams — Violet & Dawson

A friends-to-lovers, forced-proximity romantic suspense

As teens, they had a sizzling attraction they denied. Years later, they're stuck in the same house and discover nothing has changed—except the lab she's built in the garage and the secrets he's keeping. When she stumbles into his covert op, Dawson breaks old promises to keep her safe. But once he's touched her, will he be able to let her go?

Crossed by the Stars — Jada & Dax

A frenemies-to-lovers, forced-proximity suspense

Family secrets meant Dax and Jada's teenage romance was an impossibility. A decade later, the scars still prevent them from acknowledging their tantalizing chemistry. But when a shadow creeps out of Jada's past, it's Dax who shows up to protect her. And suddenly, it's hard to remember exactly why they don't belong.

Disguised as Love — Cruz & Raisa

An enemies-to-lovers, forced-proximity suspense

Cruz Malone is determined to bring down the Leskov clan for good. If he has to arrest—or bed—the sexy blonde scientist of the family to make it happen, so be it. But there's no way Raisa is just going to sit back and let the infuriating agent dismantle her world…or her heart.

The Painted Daisies

Interconnected series with an all-female rock band, the alpha heroes who steal their hearts, and suspense that will leave you breathless. Each story has its own HEA.

Swan River — *The Painted Daisies* Prequel

A rock-star, small-town, romantic suspense cliffhanger

The Painted Daisies are more than a band, they're a beloved family. With their star on the rise, life seems perfect until darkness strikes. When the group's trouble points to the band members' various secrets, it'll take strength and perseverance to unravel the mystery. Available on Amazon and also FREE with newsletter subscription.

Sweet Memory — Paisley & Jonas

An opposing-worlds, friends-to-lovers romance

The world's sweetest rock star falls for a troubled music producer whose past comes back to haunt them.

Green Jewel — Fiadh & Asher

An enemies-to-lovers, single-dad romance

Snowed in with the enemy is the perfect time to prove he was behind her friend's murder. She'll just have to ignore her body's reaction to him to do it.

Cherry Brandy — Leya & Holden

A forced-proximity, bodyguard romance

Being on the run with only one bed is no excuse to touch her…until touching is the only choice.

Blue Marguerite — Adria & Ronan

A celebrity, second-chance, frenemy romance

She vowed to never forgive him! But when he offers answers her family desperately seeks and protects her from the latest threat to the band, her resolve starts to crumble.

Royal Haze — Nikki & D'Angelo

A bodyguard, on-the-run with a morally gray hero

He was ready to torture, steal, and kill to defend the world he believed in. What he wasn't prepared for…was her.

My Life as an Album Series

My Life as a Country Album — Cam's Story

A boy-next-door, small-town romance

A first-love heartbreaker. What happens when you've pined your whole life for the football hero next door, and he finally, finally notices you? You vow to love him forever until fate comes calling and threatens to take it all away.

My Life as a Pop Album — Mia & Derek

A rock-star, road-trip romance

Bookworm Mia attempts to put behind years of guilt by taking a chance on a once-in-a-lifetime, road-trip adventure with a soulful musician. But what will happen to the heart Derek steals when their time together is over?

My Life as a Rock Album — Seth & PJ

A second-chance, antihero romance

Trash artist Seth Carmen knows he deserves to be alone. But when he finds and loses the love of his life, he still can't help sending her love letters to try and win her back. Can he prove to her they can make broken beautiful?

My Life as a Mixtape — Lonnie & Wynn
A single-dad, small-town, rock-star romance

Lonnie's always seen relationships as a burden instead of a gift, and picking up the pieces his sister leaves behind is just one of the reasons. When Wynn offers him friendship and help in caring for his young niece, he never expects love to bloom or the second chance at life they're all given.

My Life as a Holiday Album – 2nd Generation
A small-town romance

Come home for the holidays with this heartwarming, full-length standalone full of hidden secrets, true love, and the real meaning of family. Perfect for lovers of *Love Actually* and Hallmark movies, this steamy story intertwines the lives of six couples as they find their way to their happily ever afters with the help of family and friends.

My Life as an Album Series Box Set
The 1st four Album series stories + an exclusive novella

In *This Life with Cam*, Blake Abbott writes to Cam about what it was like to grow up in the shadow of her relationship with Jake and just when he first fell for the little girl with the popsicle-stained lips. Can he prove to Cam that she isn't broken?

Free Stories

Get these novellas, flash fiction stories, + bonus epilogues for
FREE with a newsletter subscription at:
https://www.ljevansbooks.com/freeljbooks

Perfectly Fine — A fish-out-of-water, celebrity romance

He's a charming, A-list actor at the top of his game. She's a determined, small-town screenwriter hoping for a deal. They form an unexpected connection until heartbreak ruins their future. Also available on Amazon.

Swan River — A rock star, romantic suspense *prequel*

The Painted Daisies are more than a band, they're a beloved family. With their star on the rise, life seems perfect until darkness strikes. When the group's trouble points to the band members' various secrets, it'll take strength and perseverance to unravel the mystery. Also available on Amazon.

Rumor — A small-town, rock-star romance

There's only one thing rock star Chase Legend needs to ring in the new year, and that's to know what Reyna Rossi tastes like. After ten years, there's no way he's letting her escape the night without their souls touching. Reyna has other plans. After all, she doesn't need the entire town wagging their tongues about her any more than they already do.

Love Ain't — A friends-to-lovers, cowboy romance

Reese knows her best friend and rodeo king, Dalton Abbott, is never going to fall in love, get married, and have kids. He's left so many broken hearts behind that there's gotta be a museum full of them somewhere. So when he gives her a look from under the brim of his hat, promising both jagged relief and pain, she knows better than to give in.

The Long Con — A sexy, antihero romance

Adler is after one thing: the next big payday. Then, Brielle sways into his world with her own game in play, and those aquamarine-colored eyes almost make him forget his number-one rule. But she'll learn—love isn't a con he's interested in.

The Light Princess — An old-fashioned fairy tale

A princess who glows with a magical light, a kingdom at war, and a kiss that changes the world. This is an extended version of the fairy tale twined through the pages of *Charming and the Cherry Blossom*.

About the Author

Award-winning author, LJ Evans, lives in Northern California with her husband, child, and the three terrors called cats. She's written compulsively since she was a little girl, often getting derailed from what she should be doing by a song lyric that sends her scrambling to jot a scene down.

A former first-grade teacher, she now spends her days deep in the pages of romance and mystery with a bit of the otherworldly thrown in. Her favorite characters are those who live resiliently, stubbornly and triumphantly getting through this wild ride called life with hope, love, and found families guiding the way.

Her novels have won multiple industry awards, including *CHARMING AND THE CHERRY BLOSSOM* which was Writer's Digest's Self-Published E-book Romance of the Year.

For more information about LJ, check out any of these sites:

www.ljevansbooks.com
FaceBook Group: LJ's Music & Stories
LJ Evans on Amazon, Bookbub, and Goodreads
@ljevansbooks on Facebook, Instagram, TikTok, and Pinterest